For the baby

VIKING

Published by the Penguin Group
Viking Penguin, a division of Penguin Books USA Inc.,
375 Hudson Street, New York, New York 10014, USA

First published in Great Britain as *Peepo!* 1981
Published in the USA as *Peek-A-Boo!* by Viking Kestrel 1983
This miniature edition published by Viking 1990
1 3 5 7 9 10 8 6 4 2

Printed and bound in Great Britain

Library of Congress Cataloging in Publication Data

Ahlberg, Janet.
Peek-a-boo!
Summary: Brief rhyming clues invite the reader
to look through holes in the pages for a baby's view
of the world from breakfast to bedtime.
1. Toy and movable books – Specimens
[1. Babies – Fiction. 2. Toy and movable books]
I. Ahlberg, Allan. II. Title.
PZ7.A2689Pe   [E]   81-1925
ISBN 0-670-83283-9   AACR2

PEEK·A·BOO!

AN ALA NOTABLE BOOK

by

Janet & Allan Ahlberg

VIKING

Baby in the morning

PEEK-A-BOO!

What can he see?

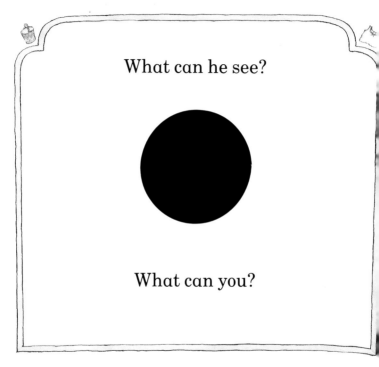

What can you?

Baby at breakfast

PEEK-A-BOO!

He can see his sisters

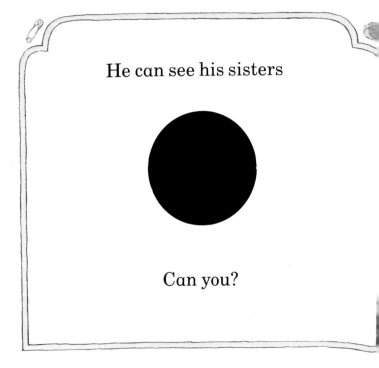

Can you?

Baby in the backyard

PEEK-A-BOO!

What can he see?

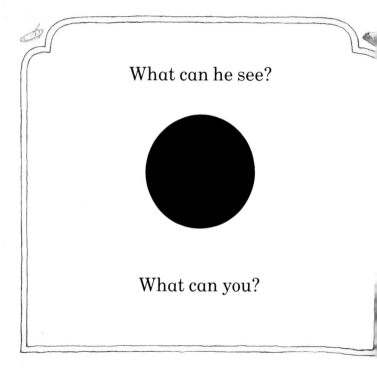

What can you?

Baby in the park

PEEK-A-BOO!

He can see three little boats

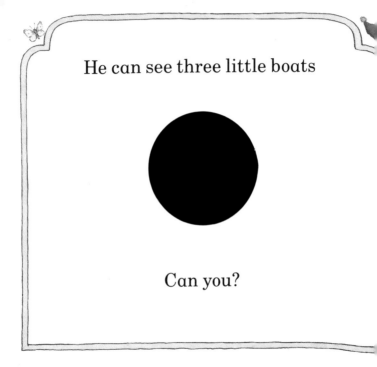

Can you?

Baby at suppertime

PEEK-A-BOO!

What can he see?

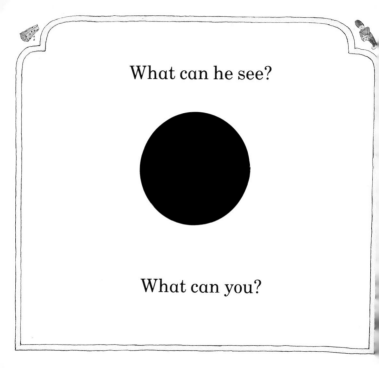

What can you?

Baby in the bath

PEEK-A-BOO!

He can see a rubber duck

Can you?

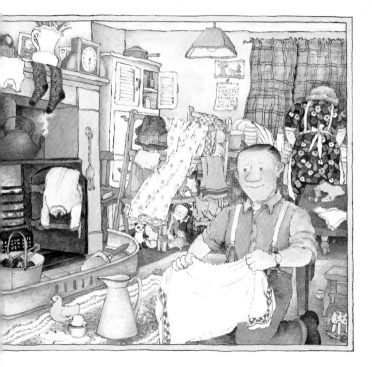

Baby at bedtime

PEEK-A-BOO!

What can he see?

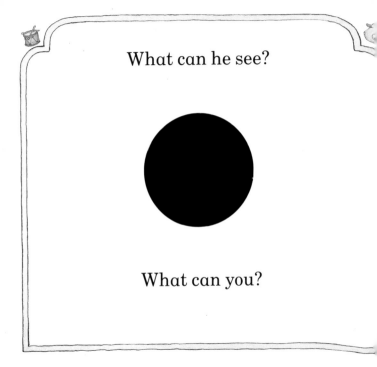

What can you?

Goodnight, Baby!

THE END